Mom, the School flooded!

story by Ken Rivard
art by Jacques Laplante

Annick Press
Toronto · New York

For Keelin, Delaney, Annie,
Melissa, Derek and Erika.
K. R.

For my sister Sylvie.
J. L.

What did you do at school today, Gus?

Oh, nothin' Mom.

NOTHING?

Weeeell...

Why are your shoes and socks and pants all wet, Gus?

Weeell, the school got flooded, and Ms. Moy and the Vice-Principal, they asked me to...

Well, we were doing geography and all this WATER came in from the hall, it kept coming...

Ms. May said we should paddle out to the gym...

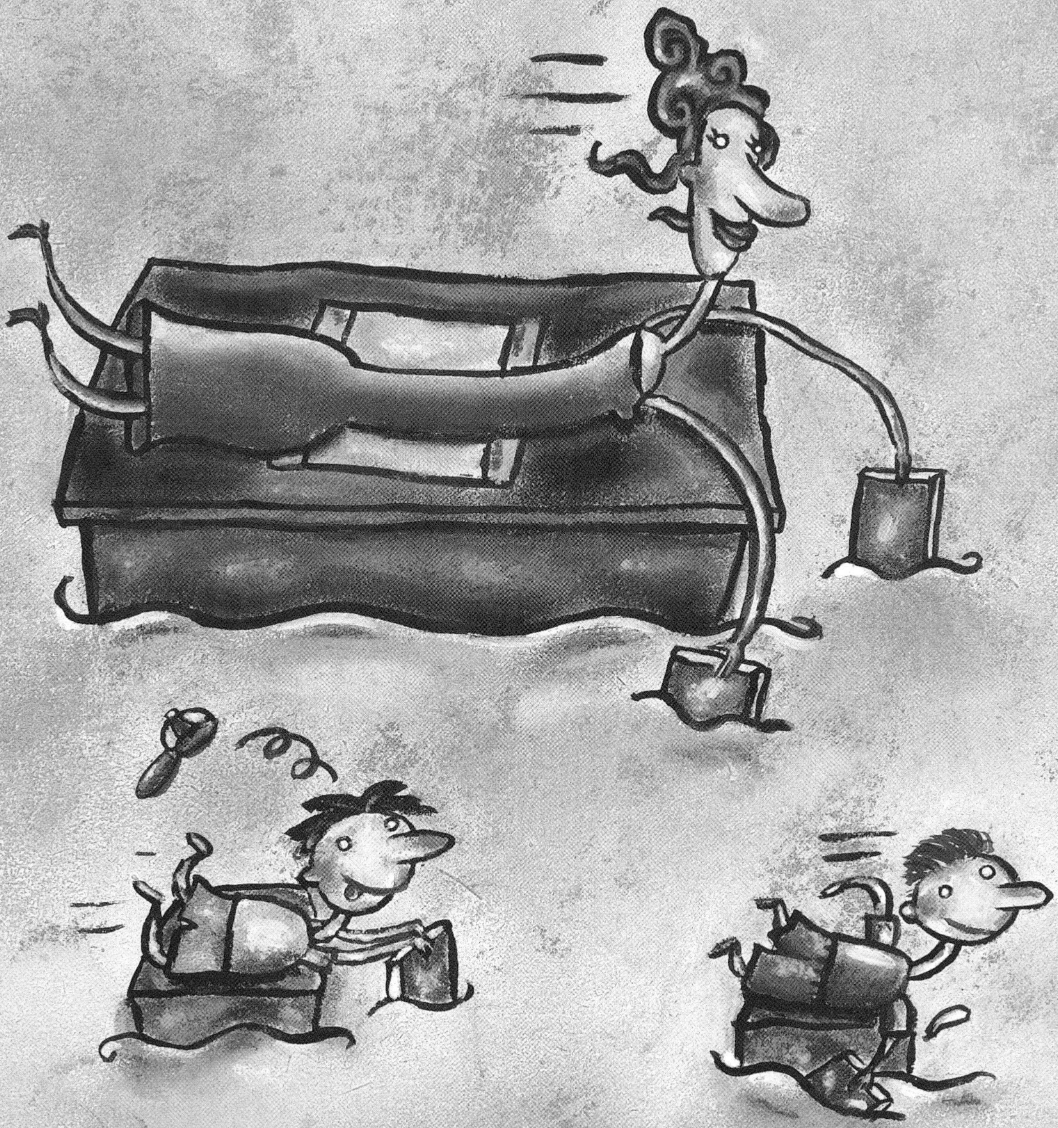

The vice-principal was calling his
Mom, I think, and then...

...he was floating in with his phone and his fish...

Gus!

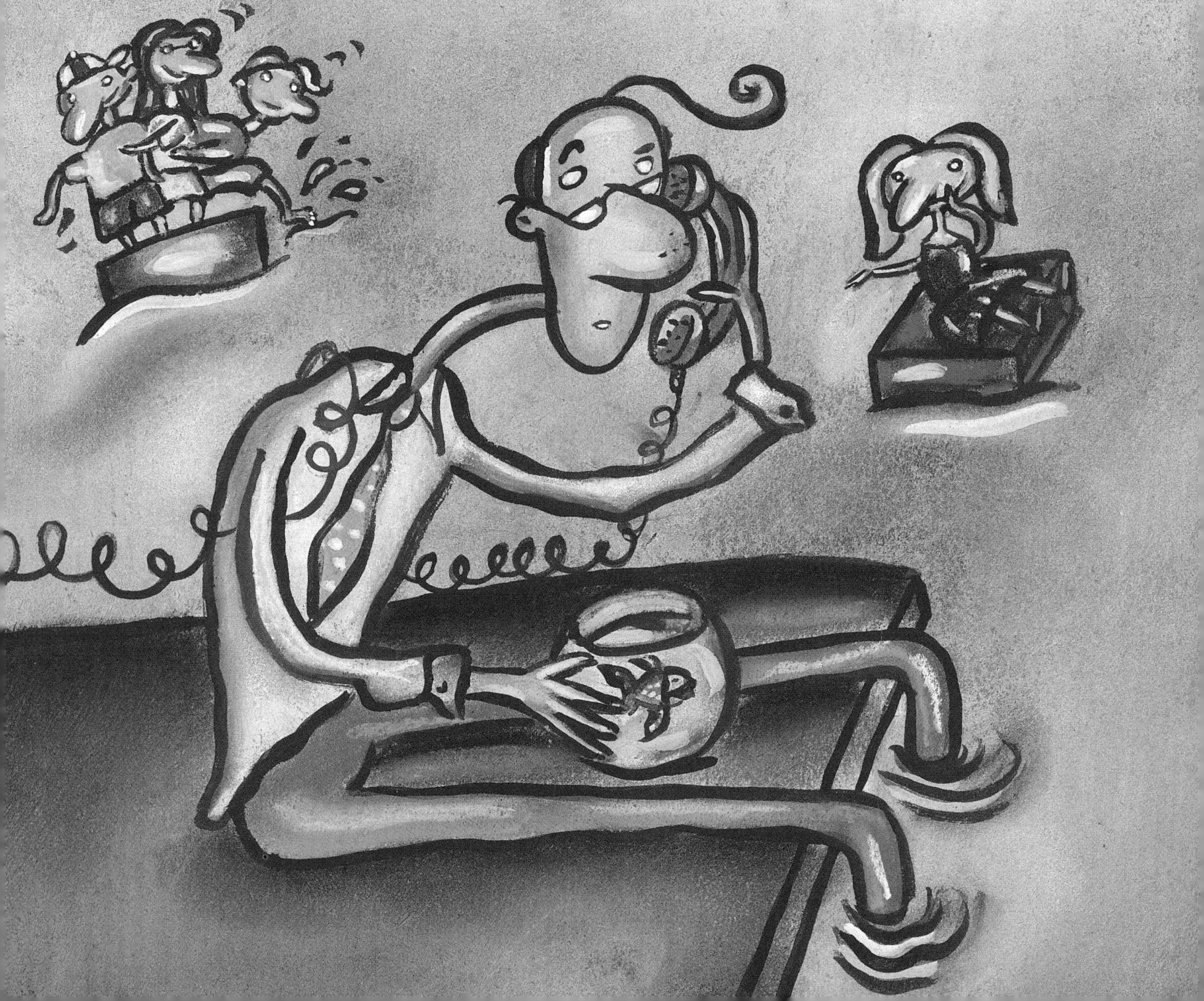

...but there was an OCEAN in the gym and...

Oh, Gus!

They opened the doors...
and the whole school yard
was flooded!

Now, Gus, honestly...

Didn't you see us on T.V., Mom?
The fire engines arrived...

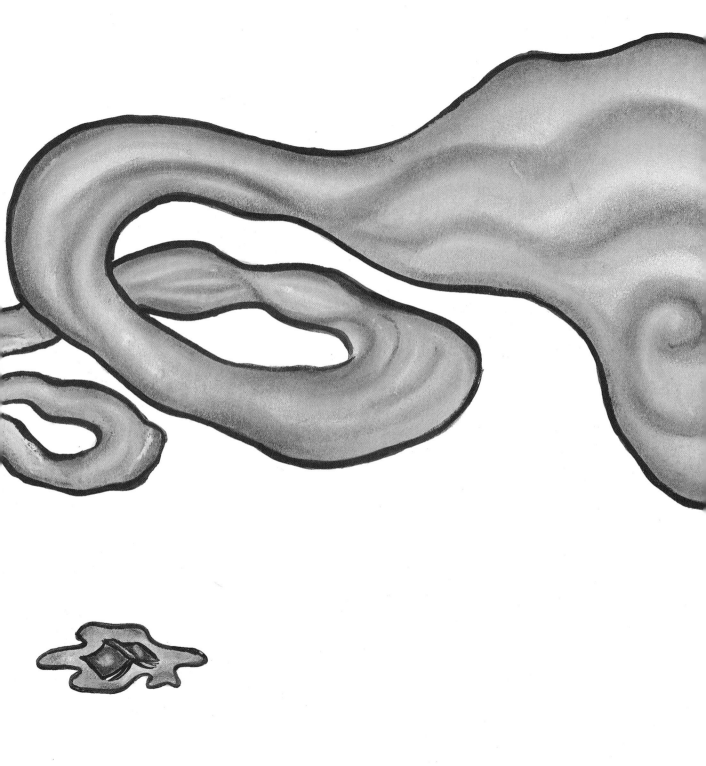

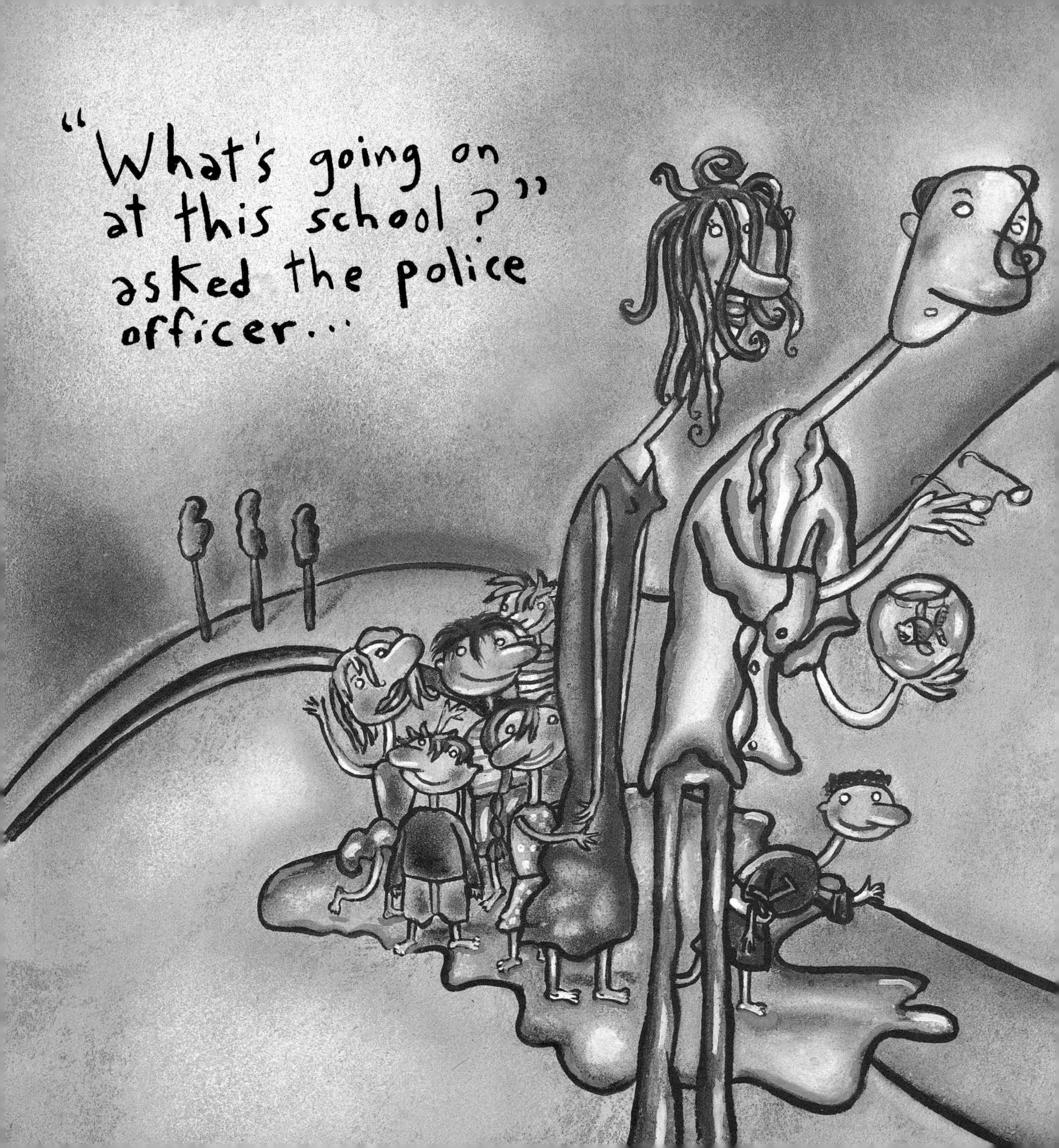
"What's going on at this school?" asked the police officer...

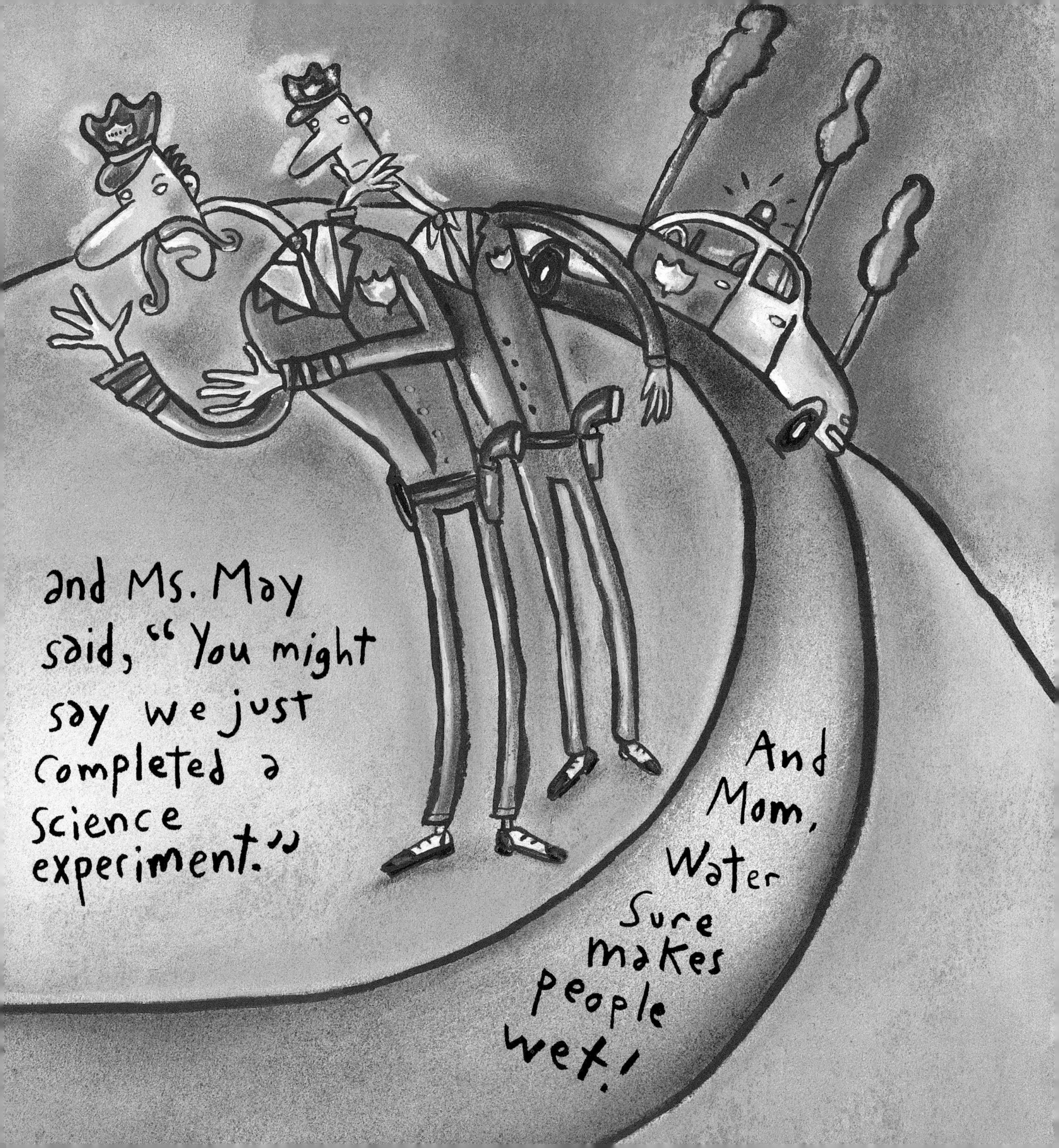

and Ms. May said, "You might say we just completed a science experiment."

And Mom, Water sure makes people wet!

DO YOU THINK
GUS'S MOM
BELIEVED HIS
STORY ?
IF YOU DO,
CLOSE THE
BOOK .
IF YOU DON'T,
TURN THE PAGE .

Okay, Mom, I was sitting quietly in the Vice-Principal's office ... when the goldfish started a fight.

DID HIS MOM
BELIEVE T<u>HIS</u>
STORY?
NO?
TURN THE PAGE.

This will shock you, Mom, but the teachers were throwing water balloons at recess - and I opened the door, and ...

Oh, Gus, let's just find some dry things for you.

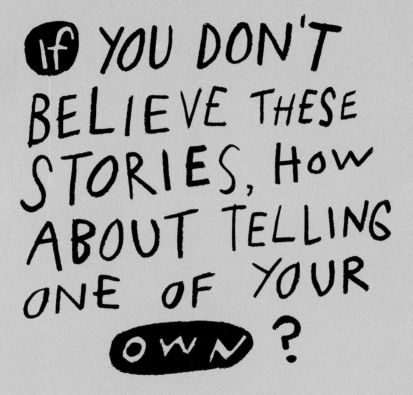

If YOU DON'T BELIEVE THESE STORIES, HOW ABOUT TELLING ONE OF YOUR OWN?

Annick Press Ltd.

Annick Press gratefully acknowledges the support
of the Canada Council and the Ontario Arts Council.

Canadian Cataloguing in Publication Data
Rivard, Ken, 1947-
 Mom, the school flooded!

ISBN 1-55037-475-3 (bound) ISBN 1-55037-474-5 (pbk.)

I. Laplante, Jacques, 1965-   . II. Title.

PS8585.I83M66 1996 jC813'.54 C95-932021-0
PZ7.R58Mo 1996

The art in this book was rendered in pastel and gouache.
The text was typeset in New Century Schoolbook.

Distributed in Canada by:
Firefly Books Ltd.
250 Sparks Avenue
Willowdale, ON
M2H 2S4

Published in the U.S.A. by Annick Press (U.S.) Ltd.
Distributed in the U.S.A. by:
Firefly Books (U.S.) Inc.
P.O. Box 1338
Ellicott Station
Buffalo, NY 14205

Printed on acid-free paper.

Printed and bound in Canada by
Friesens, Altona, Manitoba.